The Cat Flap Cats

Pamela Smyth

The Cat Flap Choir

Roger Hurn

RISING STARS

Rising Stars UK Ltd, 22 Grafton Street, London W1S 4EX

www.risingstars-uk.com

Published 2008
Text, design and layout © Rising Stars UK Ltd.

Series Consultant: Jay Mathews
Cover design: Marmalade Book Design (www.marmaladebookdesign.com)
Design: Marmalade Book Design
Publisher: Gill Budgell
Illustrations: Literacy Goes Madd

British Library Cataloguing in Publication Data.
A CIP record for this book is available from the British Library.

ISBN: 978-1-84680-372-7

Printed by: Gutenberg Press, Malta

The Cat Flap Cats

by Pamela Smyth

It's dark outside and snug in the house
And everyone's taking a nap.
But listen to the wind in the old cat flap.
And what's that strange scratching and tap-a-tap-tap?
And that shadowy shape squeezing through the gap?
Is it a dog or a cat or a little grey mouse
Coming in from the dark to our snug little house?

It's a cat called Jed.
Giant jumping Jed!
He can open his eyes to twice their size.
His favourite game is catching flies.
Once he ate six French fish pies.
Giant jumping Jed
Curls up on the bed.

Take that cat to Grandma's house,
Take it through the door!
Take that cat to Grandma's house
And put butter on its paws.

It's foggy outside and snug in the house

And everyone's taking a nap.

But listen to the wind in the old cat flap.

And what's that strange scratching and tap-a-tap-tap?

And that shadowy shape squeezing through the gap?

Is it a dog or a cat or a little grey mouse

Coming in from the dark to our snug little house?

In trots Tiger.

Fiery, wild tiger!

Her smooth fur is striped

With shadows and lights.

And her gold eyes shine bright.

Wild fiery Tiger

Climbs up on the Aga.

Take that cat to Grandma's house,

Take it through the door!

Take that cat to Grandma's house

And put butter on its paws.

It's frosty outside and snug in the house
And everyone's taking a nap.
But listen to the wind in the old cat flap.
And what's that strange scratching and tap-a-tap-tap?
And that shadowy shape squeezing through the gap?
Is it a dog or a cat or a little grey mouse
Coming in from the dark to our snug little house?

In ambles Sam.
    Fumbly, bumbly Sam!
    Plodding softly to the kitchen
    Fourteen silky whiskers twitching.
    Stops because his ears are itching.
    Bumbly, fumbly Sam
Knocks over a jar of jam.

Take that cat to Grandma's house,
    Take it through the door!
Take that cat to Grandma's house
    And put butter on its paws.

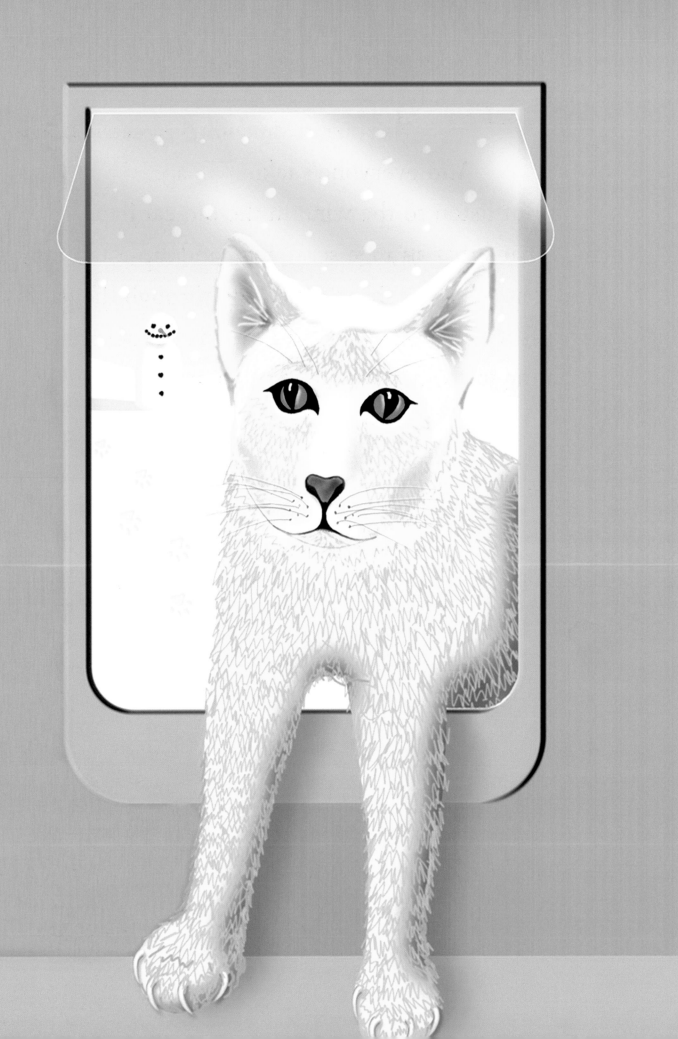

It's snowing outside and snug in the house
And everyone's taking a nap.
But listen to the wind in the old cat flap.
And what's that strange scratching and tap-a-tap-tap?
And that shadowy shape squeezing through the gap?
Is it a dog or a cat or a little grey mouse
Coming in from the dark to our snug little house?

In tiptoes Willow.
Dreamy, dainty Willow!
She can click her silver claws
And open the most difficult doors
With her clean and creamy paws.
Dreamy, dainty Willow
Pulls down a pillow.

Take that cat to Grandma's house,
Take it through the door!
Take that cat to Grandma's house
And put butter on its paws.

It's raining outside and snug in the house
And everyone's taking a nap.
But listen to the wind in the old cat flap.
And what's that strange scratching and tap-a-tap-tap?
And that shadowy shape squeezing through the gap?
Is it a dog or a cat or a little grey mouse
Coming in from the dark to our snug little house?

It's a cat called Adair.
Bouncing, baby Adair!
His tummy is round and full
His nose is a pink triangle
And his favourite toy is wool.
Baby bouncing Adair
Crawls up on the chair.

Take that cat to Grandma's house,
Take it through the door!
Take that cat to Grandma's house
And put butter on its paws.

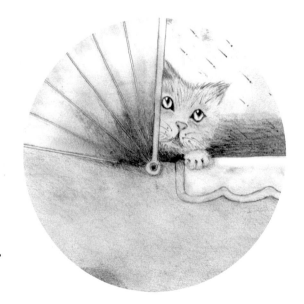

Can you imagine Grandma's house

Where the cats were sent to stay?
Is there room in Grandma's house
For cats to sleep and play?

There's little Adair sleeping on the chair.
And Willow stretched out on a bed.
Sam is enjoying a chocolate eclair.
While Tiger has her paw
on Jed's head.

But here comes
Gran's dog back
from the park
Where he goes
to ramble and roam.
He doesn't like
cats so he growls and barks
And chases the little cats home!

The Cat Flap Choir

by Roger Hurn

There is an old house
That's ramshackle and dark
It stands all by itself
On the edge of the park.
People say it's haunted
But I know that's not true.
Yet it does have a secret
Which I'll share with you.
I live in that old house
And though it's strange to say
Many cats visit me
At the end of the day.
Some slip through the cat flap
Or scratch at my door
Others slide down the chimney
And get soot upon their paws.
They all come for one purpose
They're all here for one thing
They're the Cat Flap Choir
And each one loves to sing.

Jed's the conductor
And he's so sleek and smart
He leaps right up in the air
When he wants them to start.
He waves his tail sternly
To keep time and the beat
Whilst twitching his whiskers
And tip tapping his feet.
He stands up on his hind legs
And points with both paws
Then bows from the waist
To accept their applause.
'I'm simply the best,'
Is our Jed's proud boast.
He would be if he wasn't
Tone deaf as a post.

Fat Sam miaows deeply
The windows they rattle
He fights with the tune
But it's a losing battle.
His pointy ears itch
They twitch and they shake
They'll probably fall off
From the row that he makes.

MIAOW!

Stripy Tiger she swirls

Stripy Tiger she twirls

She's a wild fiery star

With her bright golden eyes

She thinks she'll go far.

She opens up her mouth

To do her Tiger growl

But sadly her singing

Is one frightful …

YOWL!

Though little Willow's dainty
She screeches and hisses
But she thinks to herself
How wonderful this is.
Willow looks delicate
Dancing up on a crate
But her singing's as sweet
As nails scraping a slate.

HISS!

And Adair is the baby
He's a round bouncy ball
But his singing really is
The worst of them all.
He won't take singing lessons
He's too young for school
He's not the cat's whisker
Just a loud caterwaul.

SCREECH!

MIAOW! YOWL!

So when folks hurry by
My house late at night
The sound of this singing
Gives them all quite a fright.
They think that it's ghosts
Banshees and the rest
But it's the Cat Flap Choir
Just doing their best.

HISS!

SCREECH!